Keepin' It Together

Copyright © 2012 Virginia Frantz

ISBN 978-1-62141-208-3

All rights reserved. No part of this publication may be reproduced, stored in a retrieval system, or transmitted in any form or by any means, electronic, mechanical, recording or otherwise, without the prior written permission of the author.

Published by Booklocker.com, Inc., Port Charlotte, Florida.

The characters and events in this book are fictitious. Any similarity to real persons, living or dead, is coincidental and not intended by the author.

Printed in the United States of America on acid-free paper.

BookLocker.com, Inc.
2012

First Edition

Keepin' It Together

To Thelma my cousin,
I hope you enjoy this little slice of history about the Dust Bowl Days —
Love,
Virginia Frantz
July 27-2013

Virginia Frantz

Dedication

Although <u>Keepin' It Together</u> is a work of fiction, the dust storms and economic depression of the 1930's were real in the Oklahoma Panhandle. Many moved to other parts of the country to find better living conditions for their families. Others stayed behind, tied to the land through fierce family sense of ownership, or by the fact they did not have money enough to seek their fortunes elsewhere.

My parents, Bill and Virgie (Cherry) Kerns, were among those who stayed. It is to them that I pay tribute for their heroic efforts to raise their family of seven children, struggling against insurmountable odds to hold their family together through bonds of strong family values— and love.

My special thanks go to my friends and fellow Word Weaver Writers who listened patiently and offered valuable critique as I read my latest version of a chapter. These include Nicy Murphy, Meriem Nicholes, the late Bernice Halliburton, Brenda Saylor, Rachel Sides, JoAnne Graham, and especially Pamela French. Pamela has been my slave-driver, my conscience, my computer guru -- helping me out of many tight spots.

Dr. Pauline Hodges—I never would have done it if she had not taught the novel writing class that finally gave me the impetus to start turning the short stories I had hidden in my desk into chapters in this book. During this time Pauline and I have become good friends, even though she is a first class "nagger," and excuse-ignorer! Thanks to all for your help.

Last of all, I want to dedicate this book to my seven children, who with their spouses, are a blessing in my life, Jeanene Seaton, Cheryl Oquin, Nayoma Cooper, Patsy Barton, Rocky Frantz, Kara Sue Lawrence, and Clay Frantz. To each of you, thank you, for believing in me and accepting and loving me with all my foibles and quirks. You have given me pride by being loving, fair-minded, honest, and hard-working people.

What mother could ask for more?

Virginia Kerns Frantz

Chapter One: March 1937

"Ada Joyce! Ruthie!" Mama called. "Come set the table. Daddy will be home before long, and I want supper waiting for him when he gets here."

I could tell by her voice that this wasn't the first time she had called. I crawled out of my hiding place in the well-house where I went to read when I was trying to keep from having to do stuff around the house. I tucked my book, *Heidi,* under my arm and went to help Mama. Little did I dream then that when Daddy came he would be bring a letter that would turn my whole summer upside down, and most surely would limit the time I could sneak for reading.

As I entered the kitchen, Mama smiled at me and reached for the quart jar of buttermilk and poured some into the crock mixing-bowl where she was stirring up cornbread for supper.

"Where Ruthie?" she asked. "Wasn't she with you?"

"No, she and Old Shep were playing ball out by the chicken house," I said, "but she's coming."

I picked up a rag and wiped the dust from the red-checked oilcloth that covered the table. Dirt was not blowing today, but it still lingered in the air from yesterday's storm, giving everything a covering of fine dust.

Ruthie came in and washed her hands in the tin washpan that sat on the washstand along with the water bucket. As she dried her hands, she watched me solemnly when I plunked four plates on the table. Then she reached into the silverware can and counted out four each of knives, forks, and spoons. She set them down in a neat straight row by the plates, moving each plate until it sat about four inches from the edge of the table. You could have measured them with a ruler, and I bet they would all measure the same distance.

"Now," she said with a smile of satisfaction, "they are all straight."

"Ruthie, you don't have to be so careful to get everything just so. After all we're not having a banquet," I said.

"Oh, hush, Ada Joyce."

"That's just like you, Ruthie, always trying to fix things fancy, like we're the Van-Aster-Bilts of New York City. Face it, we're the Matthew Johnson family in Beaver County, Oklahoma, in the Dust Bowl, and we are dirt poor and pert near covered up with the stuff!"

Ruthie put her hands on her hips and looked up at me. "Just because we're not having company, or fixing a Sunday dinner, is no reason not to have things looking nice."

"Girls. Girls, now don't be fussing. Sisters are supposed to be nice to each other." Mama slid a pan of cornbread into the oven and stirred the bubbling beans.

"Then Ada Joyce must not be my sister," Ruthie said. We were not supposed to sass Mama, but Ruthie could get away with it.

I made a face at her, went to the front room, and picked up my book. I was really proud of that book. I'd never had my very own book before – except my schoolbooks. Mr. Whipple gave it to me for winning the spelling bee. I opened the screen door and sat down in the porch swing to read and watch for Daddy who would soon be coming over the hill "hungry as a bear," as he always told Mama.

Old Shep's cold nose nuzzled against my hand. He laid his head in my lap and looked at me with those soft brown eyes that said he knew all about me, but he liked me anyway. Ruthie says I'm bossy. Mrs. Whipple, who had been my fourth grade teacher, says that's the nature of oldest children. She says they're more apt to be leaders and usually are more responsible, but sometimes I wish I were more like Ruthie. She doesn't always have her head in a book like I do. She's nice to people and smiles at everybody, even me. She thinks she is as big as I am – and knows more. To be truthful, I'm jealous of Ruthie. She got all the looks in the family. She has a few freckles sprinkled on her nose, and her hair is dark and curly. Her eyes are as blue as the bachelor buttons that grow in Mama's garden. (Mama said flowers are food for the soul, just like carrots are food for the body.) I've got green eyes, pug nose, and straight hair the color of the straw stacks after a rain, and every summer my skin turns the color of pecan nuts.

"Mama, Daddy's comin'," I hollered when Daddy's Model A Ford topped the hill. I watched him stop at the mailbox at the corner, then chug towards home, a whitish fog of dust rising behind him. I rushed into the house, carrying my precious book with me, again calling, "Mama, Daddy's about home."

Mama smiled and removed her apron like always when she knew Daddy was coming. She looked in the mirror above the washstand and pinched her cheeks to make them red. She dampened a comb in the tin washpan, ran it through her dark, wavy hair, then tucked it into a smooth roll at the back of her head. She hurried out to meet Daddy.

I watched from the window as she and Daddy hugged and kissed like he'd been gone a month instead of just today. Mama is taller than most women, but Daddy is really tall, and he had to bend down to kiss her. He wears his dark brown hair combed back flat on his head, with a part on the left. He has a good-sized nose, which bends a little to one side.

"Emma, you sure got yourself a good looking man," I heard Martha, one of the neighbor ladies, tell Mama once.

Mama smiled and answered right back, "You're not telling me a thing that I don't already know, and you just keep your eyes to yourself, Missy." She said it teasing like, but Martha knew Mama meant business.

They came in the door, arms around each other. Daddy hung his hat on the nail behind the door, sniffed real deep, and said, "Boy, something sure smells good, I'm hungry as a bear. Brown beans, ain't it?" No matter what we're having, Daddy always acts like it's the best.

"Yes, beans and cornbread," Mama said. "I opened the last jar of pickle-lilly. I was hoping there'd be some lamb's quarter to go with them, but I looked down in the draw and didn't find any."

"Little too early for greens yet," Daddy said, "but with the shower we had night before last, we might get a mess or two in a couple of weeks, if the dirt doesn't cover them up first."

"Oh, I almost forgot. There was a letter in the mailbox for you." Daddy pulled a letter out of his pocket and handed it to Mama. "It's from your mother," He said.

Mama held it up to her cheek like she was giving Grandma a big hug. Grandma and Grandpa Geary lived in Colorado, and letters from them were pretty scarce. As Grandma warned she probably wouldn't be able to write often on account of postage was up to three cents.

I slid into a chair behind the table where I could hear better. I knew Mama would read it out loud.

> *Dear Emma, Matthew, and the Girls,*
> *Your Papa has been hired by Mr. Tucker to build a new grocery store to take the place of his that burned down. Mr. Tucker has to sell groceries from the two front rooms of their house, and they are anxious – Mrs. Tucker especially – to get the new store built – said she was tired of people traipsing in and out of her house. Papa was wondering if Matthew could come and help build the store. Papa says Matthew is one of the best carpenters he ever saw, and he would sure be obliged if he could come and help him. We thought with jobs so scarce, maybe he could use the work. He could stay with us and help Papa with the chores. It wouldn't cost him anything. The job wont be ready to start until the middle of next week because they are still cleaning up the fire mess.*

"Bless Mother's heart. She doesn't know you very well if she thinks you would stay with them and not help out on the groceries." Mama interrupted herself, then she continued reading. but I started daydreaming. I was carried away with the idea that maybe we could go, too, and live with Grandma and Grandpa and swing in the tire hanging from the big cottonwood in their yard and play with our Aunt Rena Jo, who is my age. Maybe we could help Grandma feed Maggie, the Magpie that lived in her yard and came when she called it.

When Mama stopped reading, she asked Daddy "What do you think, Matt?" knowing all the time what the answer had to be. Jobs were too scarce to let one get away.

"Emma, you know I don't want to go that far to work, but that sounds like the only chance there will be for a job anytime soon, kind of like pennies from Heaven. The commissioner says no more WPA jobs for several months. But that's a long ways away – two hundred miles – about a five-hour drive. I'd have to leave you with everything to take care of, and that would mean you'd be here without a car. Most anything you would need you could get at the store at Gray. Ada Joyce can walk that far – if she had to. If there was anything special that you needed to go to Perryton for, you could probably find a ride with the Yates."

Mama said, "We'll make out just fine, Matt. You have to do what you have to do, and I don't want anyone thinking I couldn't or wouldn't do my part. I know you helped Mr. Yates in trade for some hay and oats for the cattle and hogs. Do you suppose you all could bring it to the barn before you have to go to Colorado? If we have feed handy, the girls and I can manage. Ada Joyce is big enough to be a lot of help. Right now I can't think of a thing we would need that we couldn't get in Gray."

I looked around to see if Ruthie had heard the news, but she was on the porch, riding Shep like he was a pony. When she saw me in the door, she kissed him on the ear, whispered to him that she had to go eat supper, but she would be out to play with him later.

"Let's eat," Mama said. "Girls, wash your hands again. I saw you both playing with Old Shep."

Chapter Two: March, 1937

"Matthew, you know the mortgage payment is coming up this fall. I have been worrying how we could possibly make it, but if you took this job there would be enough for that. You really don't have much of a choice, do you think? I've been praying about it a lot, and maybe this is the answer."

I could hear Mama talking to Daddy from the other side of the partition that separated the kitchen from Ruthie's and my bedroom. Most mornings they got up early to drink coffee and visit before Ruthie and I got up. I listened every chance I got and learned a lot of stuff they wouldn't discuss in front of us kids. I knew that we owed a mortgage payment to the Federal Land Bank. I had heard them talk about it before. They talked about needing enough money saved to buy supplies for the winter.

I'd heard them talk about people who had moved away to get out of the dust storms or who had sold their farms and moved to town. They talked about folks who were sick, who were having babies, but mostly they talked about how high priced everything was, with no money to buy it. They only talk about these things when they thought we were still asleep. This morning, they kept coming back to the job offer in Colorado. I scooted up in my bed and leaned back so their voices were plainer.

"I talked to the County Commissioner yesterday," Daddy said, " and he says there won't be any more WPA road work for maybe three or four months—and no guarantee that I'll get called if there *is* work. There are ten men wanting every job that comes available. That opportunity with your daddy may be our only means of earning a little money. Granada, Colorado's a long way off though—200 miles to your folks. Sure a long way to leave your family behind. Just wish there was some way I could take you and the girls with me."

The tears started running down my face, and I wiped my nose on the pillowcase. I knew I was being a baby, but I really wanted us to go, too.

"I know," Mama, answered him softly, and I could just see her arm reach over his shoulder and her hand curl around his neck. That was a gesture she did often, and I could see it plain as day, like there wasn't a wall between us.

"Matt, I can hardly stand to see you go, but you and I have fought the Depression together, and we can't quit now. It's going to be over one of these days, but in the meantime we have to make sacrifices. You don't want to go so far away from us to work, and I hate being left behind, but I know someone has to stay here and hold the farm together. If we can hang onto the farm, it will give us something to build on when the rains start coming and money's not so scarce. We can't ask neighbors to take care of our livestock—they've got their own problems. And let's face it we can't afford for me to leave my garden. It usually feeds us all summer, and most years I can enough vegetables and plums that we have enough canned stuff to see us through the winter. If we could do what I'd like, the girls and I would go with you, but that's just not practical. And as I said before, I don't want anyone to be able to say that I wouldn't to do my part."

"That's my girl," Daddy told her. "One thing about it, you help with the chores so much that you know exactly what needs to be done. Ada Joyce can help. She's getting big enough now, and she needs to learn how to do the chores around here anyway. She likes to hide in a book too well." Daddy said.

"I do like the fact that she enjoys reading," Mama said. "But she does go a little overboard sometimes. She thinks I don't know, but she takes her book and hides out a lot."

I strained to hear what she was saying. When someone is talking about you, you sure want to hear what they've got to say!

Mama continued, "Ada Joyce is a dreamer, and I know I probably haven't been as firm about her helping me as I should have been. She *is* growing up."

They went on to talk of other things. And I sort of tuned them out. Was I a dreamer? Was that the reason I loved to read so much? I hadn't thought anyone noticed when I hid out with my book.

Daddy spoke again. "Will you be able to get by without the car?"

"Oh, sure." Mama told him, "We won't really need much in the way of groceries. We have most of the staples we'd need. We have plenty of cornmeal, flour, and sugar and have a couple of gallons of lard since you and the Freeman's butchered the hogs. The hens are laying pretty well, and we should have all the milk and cream we need. And, it won't be too long until we begin to get lettuce, radishes, and green peas from the garden. Squash won't be far behind. They look promising, if only the dust storms don't cover them up."

"Well, if you're sure you can handle things here, we'd better write and tell your folks that I'll come next week." Daddy said.

"I believe that is the only thing we can do." Mama said.

The next few days were full of a million last minute jobs. I saw Daddy and Mr. Yates go by the school one day, heading to our house with some hay and sacks of grain on Mr. Yates' old flatbed Dodge. By the time we got home from school, Daddy and Mr. Yates had most of the hay safely stashed in our barn loft. Daddy had left the sacks of oats in a granary so we could give a little to each milk cow when they came into be milked.

Daddy and Mama went to Gray one day to get some lye because Mama intended to make some lye soap. She had a crock jar of cracklings in the cellar that she collected when they rendered the lard. They bought a five-gallon can of gasoline for our Maytag wringer washer, and Mama had thought to get a box of matches for the lamps, too. We were almost out. Daddy reached in his shirt pocket and gave Ruthie and me both a little stick of peppermint candy. Daddy brought us candy every time they bought some groceries, if he had two extra pennies.

One morning as we left walking to school, Daddy was working on the Maytag's starter to make it easier to step down on to start the motor. Water steamed in the big black pot in the yard. Mama cut lye soap in the water so it would be almost melted by the time they carried the hot water to the washer.

After school there were clothes of all kinds flapping on the line. She'd even washed Daddy's carpenter overalls, and they were jumping in the breeze like they were doing some kind of fancy dance. Mama was determined that every stitch of clothes was going to be clean when they left the place. She even hung three quilts out on the line to air and fluff before she folded them up and put them in the car with the basket of Daddy's clothes that was growing taller all the time.

While she was doing all this, Daddy worked at odd jobs around the place and spent time getting his tools in top shape. He spent one afternoon sharpening his two saws, filing the two little rows of teeth with a fine file. Then he shined them with a rag dipped in coal oil. He stacked all his tools in the wooden box made for that purpose. I saw him checking them off in his head. There was a hammer, a plane, a square, a level, two saws, and his folding ruler that Ruthie and I were never allowed to touch. After he loaded the box of tools in the car, he tied the two sawhorses to the spare wheel fastened on the back of the car.

Daddy stood on the porch looking around like he was trying to memorize how the farm looked. Everything was ready for him to leave. But we weren't ready for him to go. Funny how you keep trying to hold back time, but finally the time you dread comes anyway. Mama came bringing out a box with his lunch. She had baked a hen and was sending most of it with him, along with a jar of dill pickles and fresh bread she had made, one loaf for him and one to take along to Grandma, Grandpa, and Rena Jo.

Ruthie started wailing." Daddy, don't go. Please don't go."

Daddy reached down and pulled us both to him, giving us hugs and kisses, and in between, telling me, "Ada Joyce, I am really counting on you. Ruthie is still too little to do much, but I know you can be a big help to your Mama. Look around to see what there is to do, and try to help do it. I wish I didn't have to go away to work, but right now it seems like that's the only job open." He hugged me again and said, "We're all in this as a family, trying to keep everything together. Lots of our neighbors have lost their farms. You understand how important this is?"

"Yes, Daddy." And I did understand.

I made up my mind right then that I would not hide out to read in the well-house anymore, that I really would do everything I could to do my share. I would even try not to be so bossy to Ruthie.

Ruthie still hung on to his legs with her arms and legs both wrapped around them, like she could keep him home if she just held on tight enough. He dried her tears on his red bandanna handkerchief and pulled her around in front of him. "And you, Little One, you quit your crying. You can help Mama a lot, too, just by being your sweet self. Help as much as you can. I'll be home again before you know it."

Ruthie was still taking big gulping breaths, but the tears were dry. Daddy hugged her, tousled her hair, nuzzled her neck and ears, and put her gently on the ground. He gave her a little spat on the bottom and said, "Go see if you can find Shep."

Ruthie's tears were dried, but Mama's were not. Brave as she had acted all the time they were getting Daddy ready to leave, those tears started rolling quietly down her face. He reached out and took her in his arms. She wiped them away and smiled up at Daddy.

He hugged and kissed her and said soft things to her that I couldn't hear.

"I know," she said. "I'm being such a big baby. You'd better write to us though."

"I promise." He told her. He gave her one fiercer hug and kiss and wiped his own eyes as he climbed into the little Ford car and stepped down on the starter.

On the second try, the motor caught, and he chugged slowly from the yard, looking over his shoulder, waving and blowing kisses. He headed north towards Colorado. We waved and cried as we watched him disappear over the hill.

Daddy was gone, and we were already lonesome for him.

Chapter Three: April, 1937

My first milking lesson started easy. Mama stooped down by the stool I had pulled up by Old Jersey. "See, you squeeze your thumb first, and the pointing finger, and make each finger tighter, and squeeze as it pushes the milk down and out. See?"

I tried the technique she had demonstrated. A little bit of milk came out.

"Just keep practicing that same exercise, and pretty soon it will come naturally to you." With that, Mama stood up and went to tend to Milly's milking.

I kept trying. "First the thumb and the pointing finger, then each finer and squeeze." I repeated over and over as I pulled on the cows teats, hoping to get the milk to zing into the bottom of the pail like Mama's did. Mama finished milking Milly and poured a little milk in the cats' pan. She then hung her bucket on the board Daddy had nailed sticking out from a stanchion post, and came again to stand by me.

"Not having much luck, Ada Joyce?" she asked.

"Nah, Mama, you make it look so easy. The milk fairly pours into the bucket when you're doing the milking. I can't get more than a few drops. The bottom of the bucket is barely covered, and my wrists are burning like fire."

"You'll learn," she said. "Here, hop up. I'll finish. It takes practice, and you are just starting. Remember, I've been milking cows since I was about your age. Milking takes muscles you don't need for just everything."

I thought that was sweet of Mama to try to make me feel better about my feeble attempt.

"You'll soon be milking as fast as I do," she added, over the sound of the steady stream of milk now plunking into the bucket.

I hoped so, but right now I wasn't so certain. I'd sure hate to think it would be this hard every time!

There was a loneliness going into the house at lamp lighting time, just knowing Daddy was gone and would not be home that night or any time soon. We each had another cookie and a glass of milk for supper. Then Mama read us the story of David and Goliath and listened to our prayers. Ruthie and I both prayed that Daddy had arrived safely at Grandma and Grandpa's.

In the morning after breakfast, I again tried my hand at milking, and again Mama finished milking Old Jersey for me. "You'll soon get the hang of it." She told me. "Better get ready and get to school."

I ran to the house where Ruthie had the breakfast dishes stacked in the dishpan. "Look, Ada Joyce. I fixed our sandwiches. We've got napkins. Mama told me I could cut a sugar sack in two, and now we each have a napkin to wrap our sandwich in." Ruthie unwrapped one and showed me the fried egg and biscuit sandwich she fixed from the extras Mama had cooked for breakfast. She had stuck two cookies in each of our syrup-bucket-lunch-pails, too.

"Those are great, Ruthie." She was so proud of herself for making napkins, I was determined this time I would not start a fight about her being so fixy, and trying to make everything so nicy-nice.

We bent over the washpan and splashed cold water on our faces and hands, wiping them on the towel that hung on a nail by the water bucket. We changed into our school dresses; she wore her pink flowered, and I wore my blue polka dot. We took our sweaters off the hook behind the door and grabbed up our lunch buckets. We headed across our field towards Fulton School, located the south side of our section, three quarters of a mile from our house.

The pasture was mostly bare from all the dust storms that had swept up most growing things from their path. Several sage bushes grew there still; they were a stubborn plant. Soapweeds also clung to the soil, refusing to give in to the constant winds. Only in the draw we walked through, was there any green showing. There were early starts of Lamb's Quarter and wild Dock. Tiny willow trees, not much more than ankle high, and almost as thick as grass, grew on the bottom. I helped Ruthie with the big step necessary to get on the bank from the draw.

We came to the barbed wire fence that separated Mr. Franklin's pasture from ours. I stepped on the bottom wire and pulled the middle one up so Ruthie could climb through.

"Push down on the middle one, Ruthie," I said, and eased between the middle and top wires, careful to hold my skirt away from the sharp barbs, which could easily tear skin or clothes.

Fulton School's entryway extended south of the two main rooms of the faded white, wooden building. Rose bushes grew between the sidewalk and the south wall of the building, kept alive only by Mrs. Whipple's insistence that all water from the washpan be poured on them. Tiny green leaves were just peeking from the thorny branches, growing through a blow-dirt drift. Later in the spring they would be covered in yellow roses that always smelled so sweet, but which inflicted lots of scratches on our arms and hands when we were brave enough to pick them.

We climbed the three steps into the entryway that also served as a place to hang sweaters and coats and a shelf to set our lunch buckets on, which we did. There were two schoolroom doors that opened from that first entryway. Ruthie was in the "Little Room" that held the first four grades that Mrs. Whipple taught, and I was in Mrs. Whipple's "Big Room," grades five through eight.

Ruthie giggled as she went into the 'Little Room,' where Mrs. Whipple stood at the door to give her a big hug, which was how she greeted each of her students.

I turned into the 'Big Room' where, as usual, Mr. Whipple sat behind the teacher's desk perched on the stage, a platform raised about twelve inches higher than the rest of the room. He looked over his horn-rimmed glasses and said, as he did every morning, "Good Morning, Ada Joyce, is the dirt blowing?" Like he hadn't come in out of the weather twenty or thirty minutes earlier himself.

I answered, "A little bit, Sir." But some mornings I answered, "Can't see the windmill, Sir." On other mornings it was, "Gettin' higher all the time, Sir" and once in a while, I could answer, "No, Sir. It's a calm and pretty day!"

If I said it was calm and pretty, his answer was always, "Give it a little time. The wind will be whooping it up before recess."

I suppose, unless he was teaching a class, Mr. Whipple didn't really know much what to say to kids, because he asked the other kids the same thing when they came in. "Dust blowing this morning?" But, boy howdy, when Mr. Whipple taught a class of geography, you felt you were there visiting the country and seeing the people and learning their way of life. Same way with Arithmetic. He made it a game, like some big puzzle you couldn't wait to put together. I really liked school, and so did most of the other kids.

Whatever the weather was doing would not make any difference about cleaning to Mr. Whipple. He did not believe in sweeping, "because it would have to be done again tomorrow." He refused to fight with the wind, he told everyone. As a result, the silt-like dirt came into the big room and stayed undisturbed, as one dust storm followed another, depositing one layer of the brown powder on top of the last, and now we walked on two or three inches of pure dirt. Nearly every morning we wiped dust or blew it off our desks.

When each teacher signed his or her contracts, they agreed to sweep the floors and keep the big heating stove going in cold weather. He kept the room warm. He would send two boys to carry in the coal or carry out the ashes as "an honor for being extra good" or "for making a higher grade than they usually did." He always found some way to reward the boys, but no one wanted to be rewarded enough to get to sweep the floor or scoop it out. Mr. Whipple always said, "Dust underfoot never stifled anyone's learning." I was real proud of Mrs. Whipple; she swept her floor every day and helped him some with grading, but she never swept his floor.

I didn't hear any grownups in the community fault him for it, except Mrs. Lowman, the wife of the school board president. She had plenty to say. She said, "It behooves anyone who makes the high dollars that Mr. Whipple does to do everything in his contract to earn his sixty-five dollar a month salary!" But I never heard of it coming up in a school board meeting.

The hour hand on the wall clock showed nine o'clock, and Mr. Whipple picked up the bell from his desk and rang it to indicate that we were officially in school. He called the roll as he did every day. As usual my friend Johnnie Jorden was late. He and his little brother Pee Wee had to walk two and a half miles to school and more times than not, they got there after the bell had rung.

My name was top on the board, so that meant it was my turn to lead the morning exercises. I went to the front and led everyone in the Pledge of Allegiance, and the Lord's Prayer. Next we sang, "Good Morning To You." I returned to my seat and Mr. Whipple started writing our arithmetic test on the board. School had begun for the day.

Johnnie eased the door open and slipped into his seat behind me. But Mr. Whipple heard him or saw him reflected in his glasses. Mr. Whipple turned and looked over his glasses at Johnnie, but he didn't scold him for being late. He just said, "Good Morning, Johnnie. Is the dust blowing?"

Now school had started.

Chapter Four: April 1937

"Here, turkey, turkey, turkey," I called, sliding down from the windswept, barren pasture into the draw. Small willow trees were growing knee high and so thick that I mashed some with every step. This morning at breakfast, as Mama shook some chocolate pancakes on my plate, she brought up the subject of the missing turkey.

"Ada Joyce, as soon we get the washing started, I wish you'd go see if you can find where that turkey hen has hid her nest. I'd go help hunt, but for the first time all week the wind's not blowing. I just have to get the washing done. You girls are out of clean clothes to wear to school.

I had helped Mama build a fire under the black kettle in the yard and carried water from the well house to it fill it up. As soon as the water was hot and the slivers of lye soap melted, I filled the Maytag with the soapy water. She was cranking on the gasoline motor when I set out for the pasture. Soon I heard the pop, pop, pop, of the motor and knew that Mama's trusty machine was doing its work.

"Here, turkey. Here, turkey." I called again, brushing the short weeds aside. Last night the coyotes howled close by, and that was one reason Mama was so anxious to find the turkey and her nest. We had gathered the eggs from nests of the turkeys who had made nests close by. Mama would put a hen's egg in each nest she found so the turkey hen would still be under the impression that her nest was well hidden. Mama kept those eggs in the cellar, keeping them fresh until she could get enough turkey eggs gathered to put under her broody Rhode Island Red chicken hens. She had three of her chicken hens setting on turkey eggs now. But this old biddy I was looking for today was being sneaky and trying to hatch her own babies.

Each turkey Mama saved meant a lot to her. They were her own special project to help with family finances. Each fall, right before Thanksgiving, she and Daddy would catch the turkeys, put them in cages, and take them to town to sell. She used the money to buy Ruthie or me a winter coat, any needed groceries we were out of, plus she bought presents for us, which she always managed to hide from us until Christmas.

A little jack rabbit jumped up right at my feet, scaring me as much as if it was a bear, but it did bring my thoughts back to what I was supposed to be doing. I let my pounding heart slow a little then continued on.

"Here, turkey, turkey, turkey." I sneezed as I parted the pungent-smelling fronds of a blue sage bush. A big rock jutted out from the bank of the draw, but the turkey's nest was not under there, either. A few steps farther on, a little cottonwood tree was trying to get a start. I pushed aside the little twiggy branches and…"Gotcha!" Ruthie hollered, laughing like she had pulled the greatest joke possible. Old Shep was right behind her, looking as if he was laughing at her joke.

"Betty Ruth!" I hollered. "You scared me! How come you to slip up on me like that? You nearly gave me a heart attack."

Ruthie thought the whole situation was funny. But I didn't.

"Why'd you come down in the pasture by yourself? Did Mama say you could?"

"Didn't ask her," Ruthie said, real sassy like. "Sides, I wasn't by myself, 'sides Old Shep came with me."

"We sure don't need old Shep." I told her. "If we do happen to find the Mama hen, he'll scare her. But anyway, I heard Mama tell you to wash the dishes. Do you have them done?"

"Nope," she answered, "No hot water."

"Couldn't you fill the tea kettle and put it on the burner?"

"No, the water bucket is empty."

"Ruthie, I never heard such a sorry excuse. All you gotta do is turn on the faucet over the water bucket on the washstand. It might take 10 or 15 minutes to fill it, but it's not like you have to go carry the water into the house. You do know how to turn on a faucet don't you? Ruthie, sometimes I think you just play dumb. No one could be as dumb as you act!"

Ruthie giggled like I had given her a big compliment, or else said something funny. She can usually get anything she wants with that cute little laugh, and I guess she can with me, too, because I said, "Come on then, Stay close. I've got a hard enough job trying to find a stupid turkey, without having to keep a little sister tagging along or keep from getting lost."

"Shep's a good hunter. He'd find me," Ruthie said, as if that settled the matter.

Ruthie fell in behind me as I walked on down the draw, looking under the sagebrush and dodging the sharp spears of the soapweeds as I looked behind them. Shep walked back and forth around us, only his back showing above the little willows.

"Keep right behind me, Ruthie," I told her, trying to part the little willow trees so they wouldn't scratch her legs when she came through. "Here, turkey, turkey, turkey" I called.

"Here, turkey, turkey, turkey," Ruthie echoed.

I stopped and put my hand behind me to stop Ruthie too. "Be real quiet," I told Ruthie. "There's something ahead," I whispered.

"Is it the turkey?" Ruthie whispered back.

I stood real still, trying to see what was moving the bushes ahead. "Ruthie! It's a skunk! Stay back." We started backing up quietly when the mama skunk waddled into a clear spot, followed by a string of wobbling baby skunks.

Curious Shep circled toward them. "Shep. Come back! Come here!" I might as well have been talking to the moon. Shep ignored me like I wasn't even there and jumped at the mama skunk, barking.

"Come back, Shep," I hollered, but it was too late, the damage was done. That old mama skunk just turned around, raised her tail, and sprayed Shep full blast right in the kisser. The air was thick with a fog of the horrible smell. Shep howled and cried in pain. He ran in circles, wiping his head in the willows, rubbing first one side than another. He rolled over and over trying to clean himself of the awful stench. His eyes were watering like someone had turned on a faucet.

"Come on, Ruthie, let's get out of here." I grabbed her hand and went flying for the house, half carrying and half dragging Ruthie. Shep was right beside us.

"Stay. Shep, stay! Cover your nose, Ruthie," I said, as I swooped up my dress tail to cover my nose with my other hand. I couldn't say that helped any. The stench was part of the very air we were breathing.

"Oh, that's awful," Ruthie said bursting into tears.

"Yes." I answered, hanging on tighter when she stumbled and would have fallen if I hadn't kept a strong hold, "Keep running as fast as you can." Shep stayed right with us, trying to wipe the vile stuff on our skirts.

"Stay! Shep. Stay!" I hollered again. "Come on Ruthie, hang on. Quit bawling. It won't help" Shep acted like he had never heard the word "Stay" before. He stuck with us like glue -- crying and moaning and acting plum miserable, acting like we could do something to get the misery away from him.

We were almost to the barn when Mama heard the commotion and saw us. She dropped the basket of wet clothes she was carrying to the clothesline and ran towards us yelling, "Girls, are you all right?" When she knew we weren't hurt but just scared and stinky, she hollered again. "Don't come to the house. I don't want that stink in there. Get in the calf shed and throw your clothes out the window. They'll have to air out before I can even wash them. I'll bring some water to wash you off." We dodged into the calf shed, locking Old Shep outside, who was still crying and trying to get the stinky stuff out of his eyes. "Come on, Ruthie. I'll help you get your clothes off. Hold your breath when I pull them off, then the smell won't seem so bad." Then I stripped my clothes off, and we threw them out through the opening that used to be some windows. Almost as soon as we were bare, here Mama came, bringing the little red wagon with two cream cans full of the soapy wash water, several quarts of her home-canned tomato juice, a gallon of vinegar, and two bars of lye soap, plus some rags to wash with, and our clean clothes. She let us wash ourselves first, and then she took over. Ruthie and I hadn't had a bath from Mama in a long time but that did not stop her today. She was going to do the job right. She first bathed us in the tomato juice.

"That's supposed to help kill the smell." She said. Next, she slathered Ruthie with the lye soap and smeared it all over her. Ruthie started bawling again. "That stuff burns!" she said.

"Quit being such a baby!" I told her. Then Mama gave me the same treatment. I didn't have a spot on me that wasn't smeared with soap. "Ouch, Mama, stop. That stuff burns!" I told her. She didn't pay me any mind, just scrubbed, from the top of our heads to the bottom of our feet. She scrubbed. Didn't matter one bit how much Ruthie or me howled, Mama kept scrubbing. She didn't quit until our skins were the color of her canned pickled beets. By that time Ruthie was really blubbering, and I was hollering. "Mama, can't you stop now. My skin feels like I got in the nettle patch."

Mama ignored me and then added. "I'm going to get some water from the horse tank to rinse you off."

Ruthie and I both yelled when she doused us with the cold stuff. But only then did she seem satisfied with the results.

"Now, I've got to get that nasty dog cleaned up," she muttered, "You kids get dried off good. You could take a cold from all this bathing outside. Then another thought seemed to occur to her, the reason for our adventure. She turned to me and asked, "Did you find the turkey?" With that I felt the fright from the skunks, worry about Old Shep, the responsibility of getting Betty Ruth safely home, and the frustration that I could not find the turkey's nest, nor the turkey. I broke into a howling, bawling fit.

Mama looked at me bewildered. She was used to Ruthie bawling, but not me, I never bawl, not until today.

"What is the matter?" She asked.

I couldn't really tell her. Here I had promised Daddy I would do everything I could to help keep things together while he was gone. And I'd messed up on a simple thing like finding a turkey.

All at once, Mama seemed to understand. She hugged me and said, "Don't cry, I'll try to help you hunt the next time. We're going to find that old biddy, however long it takes!"

Chapter Five: April 1937

"Ada Joyce, you girls play with the twins, and I'll help your mom get dinner on the table," Aunt Rose said, tying one of Mama's aprons over her Sunday dress. Aunt Rose and Uncle Duval and the twins had brought us home from church and were staying for Sunday dinner. We had walked to church held in the Fulton school, and now the twins were hiding behind their mother's skirt. Ruthie and I started playing peek-a-boo with them until their mama started off to the kitchen, the twins still clinging to her skirt-tail. We followed, teasing them, and they soon warmed up to us, and we took them into the front room to play.

"Can you smell skunk on the girls?" I heard Mama ask Aunt Rose. Earlier I had heard her telling Aunt Rose about our skirmish with the skunk. She seemed to see something funny about it now, but she sure hadn't been laughing yesterday.

"I thought I got a whiff of skunk when Ole Shep came to meet us as we drove up in the yard, but I don't smell any now at all," Aunt Rose said. "Maybe a little scent left on the dog."

Uncle Duvall chuckled and said as he left the house, "Well, I'd better go fix that hinge on the barn door you told me about. That skunk might decide to take up residence there."

"Heaven forbid," Mama laughed as she scooped up the homemade noodles and dropped them in the pot where the hen had been stewing all morning while we were at church.

"We have to find that turkey hen, skunk or no skunk," Mama said. "Every turkey egg we save may mean one more turkey to sell this fall. I thought I'd go with the girls to look next time. Maybe we'll have time one day this week after school." Mama sure enjoyed having a woman to visit with, and Aunt Rose seemed to be full of the neighborhood gossip. The twins were so funny, tumbling over each other like two little tumblebugs. Ruthie and I got down on the floor to play with them and tuned out the woman talk going on in the kitchen until I heard Mama raise her voice.

"Ada Joyce, one of you girls run and tell your uncle that dinner is ready," Mama called. Ruthie jumped up and ran out the door before anyone had a chance to say anything else.

"She won't have to call him twice," Aunt Rose said. "He thinks your noodles are the best, and that coleslaw is soooo good, I snitched a bite."

Uncle Duval eased in the screen door, with Ruthie just behind, and said, "Somethin' sure smells good in here."

"I'm going to fix the twins' plates while you wash up." said Aunt Rose.

After she put noodles on saucers, she put the dishes on a chair for the twins to stand beside while they ate.

The rest of us found seats around the table, then Mama asked Uncle Duval to say the blessing.

"Lord, we're comin' to you today, thankin' you for all our blessins; one of them is this beautiful day with no wind and dirt blowin'. Lord we don't want you to think we're ungrateful and complainin', but could you send some rain for our thirsty ground? We'd sure thank you for it. Lord we ask your blessin's on members of the community that has had to go other places to try to find work. Bless them and keep them safe. We thank you now for the good lookin' food that's spread before us. Bless the food and the hands that prepared it. All these favors and blessin's we ask in Your name. Amen"

All of us dived in to a scrumptious meal of chicken and noodles, mashed potatoes, coleslaw, and for dessert we had chocolate gravy, which is my favorite dessert. Uncle Duval ate like he hadn't had anything to eat for a week. Aunt Rose sort of apologized for him, and Mama said, "Well he's been doing a lot of work around here. A working man needs to eat."

Uncle Duval smiled and said, "I see there's some boards loose on the side of the barn. There's a few nails out there in a jar so I'll see about nailing them down. With the wind whooping it up all the time, it's a wonder any of us have a barn or chicken house left standing. We're going to get some rain some of these days, and then maybe some jobs will open up closer to home. How's Matthew's project in Colorado coming along? Will he have work for quite a while?"

"They figured it would take about two or three months, but he says now there may be a possibility they can do another job while he is up there. I'll admit this is no game to stay home and try to keep everything together. I couldn't do it if the girls didn't pitch in and help like they do. Would you have some more chocolate pudding?" Mama asked.

"Naw, Uncle Duval said, "I've eaten enough for three guys already." With that he got up from the table and rubbed his stomach and gave the women a sheepish grin.

"Emma, you are one fine cook. I can sure see why Matthew would hate to be away from your table. You cook good, too, Rose." He threw in, so Aunt Rose wouldn't get her feelings hurt. "You ladies get caught up on your visiting. I'm going to go try to earn my dinner," he added as he left the house.

After he left, Aunt Rose and Mama did the dishes, chattering a mile a minute. Ruthie and I played with the twins until it was time for their naps. You could hear the hammer banging on the boards as Uncle Duval fixed the barn. When he came in, saying it was time to go, the sun was low in the West and it was chore time, much too late to look for the turkey and her nest.

Chapter Six: April/May, 1937

Monday when we arrived at school, we could tell there was something exciting going on. Maycie came running up, saying, "Ruthie, Mrs. Whipple is handing out parts for the last-of-school program. The girls in our grade are going to sing in the Spring Flower Chorus, and we're going to be different flowers and have costumes and everything. I'm going to be a sunflower," she said. "I'm going to have yellow petals."

Mrs. Whipple spotted Ruthie. "How would you like to be a daisy? We'll make pretty white petals to fit around your face, green leaves to go over your shoulders, and then everyone will have green crepe paper skirts."

Two other girls crowded around Mrs. Whipple and were given the roles of being a buttercup and a bluebell. All of them danced around, talking at once. Mrs. Whipple tried to shush them, but she finally spoke loud enough to get their attention, "Girls. Girls, you need the sheet of instructions I wrote for you to take home. Your mothers can see how to help make your skirts so they'll all be alike. Now don't forget to pick up your green crepe paper, too. I've measured enough for each skirt and put them in separate bundles."

"Do we have to buy anything?" Ruthie asked anxiously.

"No, it's all furnished," Mrs. Whipple assured her. I wondered if she knew that Mama only had two dollars and thirty-seven cents in the money can setting on the shelf above the stove. I went on to the big room to see if Mr. Whipple was assigning our parts. He was. He looked up and nodded at me.

"Good morning, Ada Joyce, is the dirt blowing?"

But before I could answer, he said, "We are going to present an all-student play for the last of school program. It will be a play school; we have decided you will be the teacher since you are the tallest, and you will announce the poems and songs the other students recite."

Why did I have to be so tall? Maybe if I wasn't, I wouldn't always have to play the part of teacher, aunt, or grandma in a play. Sometimes

I would like to be a princess, or a flower or something fun like Ruthie gets to be.

Mr. Whipple looked over his glasses and smiled at me. "But before that play starts we want you to do a reading. You have good stage presence, and it's different. See the name of the poem? It's called 'Mary Ann, Did You Pass?' We would rename it "Ada Joyce, Did You Pass? Would you be interested in doing this part?"

Of course I would! I could hardly contain my excitement. With that last comment, he reached for the bell and rang it.

"Ah, Johnnie, you're here early. Is the dirt blowing?" Mr. Whipple said, as he set the bell back on the desk.

I was surprised to see Johnnie. We hadn't even started school yet, and here he was, his grin spreading clear across his face.

After the opening exercises were finished and we were seated again, Johnnie nudged me and leaned up to whisper, "I gotta surprise."

I shook my head to shush him because Mr. Whipple would make us stay in at recess if he caught us talking. Johnnie couldn't wait to tell his surprise though, so in a minute I felt a tap on my elbow, and he slipped me a note that read. "Me and Pee Wee got new bikes! My brother Charley bought them for us."

Oh boy! A bike! I didn't know Charley was rich! Charley was Johnnie's married brother who lived in Liberal, Kansas, forty miles north of us. He had a good job, working for the city in the water department. I thought that was mighty nice of Charley, and I figured that would be the end of Johnnie and Pee Wee being late to school all the time. Still I couldn't help being envious and wishing I had a brother. But right now, I had to finish my arithmetic and hand it in.

The recess bell rang and Johnnie rushed outside so he could show off his new bike. All of us kids hurried after him, almost tumbling over each other.

"Come on, I'll give you a ride," he hollered over his shoulder to me. "You little kids stay back!" I kind of thought Johnnie was showing everybody I was his girl and that proved it.

He brought the bike up to the cement steps and told me to step on the lowest one and slide on to the handlebar. I did.

"You little kids stand back," he said and he shoved off with me precariously perched atop the bars. Somehow, I had not sat straight and we became over balanced and almost toppled over, but Johnnie put his feet down, and the bike stayed upright. Mr. Whipple, who had just come outside, hollered for us not to do that again. "It's too dangerous to ride double," he called.

I was disappointed, but Johnnie said real low, "I'll still teach you how to ride the bike anyhow."

We all stayed after school to read through our parts for the program, then rushed home so I could help Mama with the evening chores.

The next day Johnnie brought his bike and began teaching me how to ride. He showed me the best way to hold the bike steady while I swung one leg over. Then he gave me directions for riding, "Keep the wheels going in a straight line. I'll try to help you balance at first, but after I turn loose, if you start to fall, just turn your wheels."

With that full set of instructions, I took off. He ran beside me, holding the bike upright, yelling, "Hold straight! Don't get overbalanced! Steady! Steady!"

The bike plunged down the hill and zipped ahead so there was no way he could run fast enough to keep up. "Keep it straight. Keep it straight!" He hollered from behind me.

I tried to avoid a little rock in the middle of the road. The bike headed straight for the ditch.

"Turn the wheels. Turn the wheels," Johnnie yelled.

I did. But the bike and I fell into the ditch, which was full of blow dirt.

Johnnie tried not to laugh, but I know I was a funny sight with dust all over me especially in my hair. I might have laughed, too, but I had landed hard on my bottom.

"When I told you to turn the wheels, I meant turn them towards the way you're falling," he said.

"Now you tell me." I answered, half laughing and half crying. I wiped the dirt off my skinned knees and got to my feet. For the next two weeks during recesses Johnnie helped me practice riding. I soon kept the bike steady with hardly a wobble at all. In fact, Johnnie said I rode it almost as good as him.

While I was learning to ride the bike, we were also learning our parts for the program. One evening about a week before the program, Ruthie and I scurried home across the pasture. We talked about our practice and the upcoming program , thinking of everything but the lost turkey hen, and that's when we saw her. That cagey turkey was surrounded by a bunch of little poults. She was scratching and chirping to her little ones, but at the same time she kept a wary eye out for any sign of danger.

"Let's try to drive her to the house, Ruthie," I said.

"Okay," Ruthie answered, and walked quietly to the other side of the little family. We edged the hen and her babies towards home, moving slow and easy so as not to scare them.

The turkey took a few steps towards the house, all the while she nervously looked around to make sure we were not going to harm her poults. Suddenly, she marched quickly, and called her babies to follow. .She had only gone a few steps when she squawked loudly, took a couple of leaps, flapped her wings, and took to the air, sailing back over our heads like an eagle. She landed in the draw among some sage bushes and dock weeds. Her poults scurried behind her, turned like members in a practiced fire drill-team. They all disappeared in the bushes.

Ruthie started crying, and I told her, "Come on, Ruthie. Don't cry. It is a disappointment, but at least we know she's here and she has some little ones. But we don't have time to mess with them now. We've got to get home so I can get the chores done."

Still, I was disappointed that we couldn't drive the little rascals home to Mama and if I wasn't the big sister, I would cry too.

Chapter Seven: May, 1937

"Mama, do we have any magazines around here to read? I've looked at the Sears Roebuck catalog so many times out in the outhouse, that I could tell you what pages the farm tools are on," I said.

"I think I have something you'd rather read than anything. I got a letter from Daddy yesterday." Mama said.

"A letter from Daddy!" Ruthie jumped up and down. "A letter from Daddy!"

"Why didn't you tell us last night?" I asked Mama.

"Actually, I was keeping it for myself. It refers to some news I had not planned to tell you girls yet," she answered. "But you are getting to be big girls now, and I think you should know. Here's the second page," Mama said handing the pages to me.

When I saw the front page was missing, I looked at her question like, she just smiled and said, "First page later."

I started reading it to myself, but Ruthie said, "Read it to me, too." So I read starting at the top of the page Mama handed me, even if it appeared to be in the middle of a sentence.

. . .know how much longer it will be before I can come home, but it can't be too soon to suit me. There's one thing about it, the building is beginning to look more like a store every day, and every day I'm one day nearer coming home. And I am getting some of the things we must have to live on. I reserved 500 pounds of flour Thursday for $1.60 a hundred weight. Mr. Tucker told me I could do that and then get it right before I come back to Oklahoma, as it will be new wheat and freshly milled. Mr. Tucker says I was lucky, as it will be $2.15 a hundred on Monday. This evening before I left, he told me I'd better buy a sack of sugar this week, too. If I bought a 100 pounds now the price would be $4.55, but on Monday the price goes up to $5.25, so I went ahead and bought 100 pounds this evening. Now we at least have flour and sugar, if I can just get it home.

Daddy Geary just came in from delivering the milk. He said they told him at the store that beans would be higher by $1.00 a sack on Monday. Beans are $3.50 a hundred now, so Monday that will make them $4.50. I'll probably go ahead and get a hundred pounds tomorrow before the price goes up. That means I'll only have $1.50 to send you this week. Seems like everything is going up, and no work or money sure makes it hard on poor folks. Supper is ready so will stop and eat and hope to finish this in a day or two.

HELLO AGAIN, Well here it is Sunday morning, cloudy and cool. We have had about an inch of rain this past week, the Lamar paper said. Sure hope it rained some down there, too, as I know you always say a rain helps the garden more than watering by hose does.

The cow we gave the salts to last week is not well yet. She has a little calf now, but feels so bad she don't hardly notice it. Sure hope they don't lose her as your folks depend on the milk money to help keep them in groceries.

It is time to go to church now, but maybe I can write some more this evening and mail this tomorrow. I did get the beans, so that will be a lot of good eating this winter.

It's Sunday night now. It has been a good day -- well, as good as it can be when I'm away from my family. It cleared off about noon, and then after church, your two married sisters, Beth and Martha, was here with their husbands and babies. Us men played ball this afternoon. There was Daddy Geary, your brother in laws, Harry and John and me all played. We played with one of them softballs, and you know me, I like a game of any kind of ball. Ha. Ha. The women visited in the house. It is time to go milk so will try to write a few more lines later. I sure wish you could have been here today, not only today but every day.

LATER SUNDAY NIGHT I have just had supper. Your brother Del and his wife and baby are here. Daddy Geary and your little sister, Rena Jo, went down to Clark's for Bible Class. Please take it as easy as you can and tell the girls I am mighty

proud of them for helping you so good. Remember, I'll get home as soon as I can -- sooner if I need to. Well, I must close with love to you all.
Your Matthew.

I finished the last page of Daddy's letter and looked at Ruthie who was standing right next to me. "I wish Daddy was home," she said, her eyes brimming.

"Ruthie, we all do," I told her and wiped the tears running down her face. Mama held out her arms to both of us and hugged us tight.

"We ALL do," she repeated, "but we're all working to help out the family. Now, would you like to read the other page of Daddy's letter to see that it is even more important to help?"

I took the letter Mama handed me. "You can read it out loud, too," Mama said. When I read the sweet talk he started the letter with, I told her "Daddy was writing this to you, not me and Ruthie."

"Just read on," Mama told me.

April 22, from the Geary home
At Granada, Colorado
My Dear Sweet Wife,
Your letter filled me with more love than ever for you. What exciting news to know there will be another little one in our lives. I am so sorry that I can't be in both places at once.

"Mama! Does this mean you're having a baby? Are we going to have a little brother or sister?" I asked Mama.

Mama nodded silently to say that was right. Ruthie didn't say anything, just walked over to Mama and leaned against her. She put her thumb in her mouth. She hadn't done that for a long time.

I sat there quiet like and thought about the news. It was exciting news, but I had heard Mama and Daddy talking about money when they didn't know I was around listening. I read on.

The Dr. will need to be paid. You know that as much as I need this job and the money it provides, there is no way I would have come up here to Colorado and left you with all the responsibility and work of holding the place together had we known about the baby before I left. I am glad Ada Joyce is helping so good with the outside chores. She is growing up a lot to put a book down to help. That girl does love to read. You seldom see her but what she's got her head in a book. You tell her I'm mighty proud of her.

Please, Dear, do let me know if I should come home. Maybe there would be a chance of finding a job around there. You tell me that you and the girls are making it just fine, but I worry that you are not feeling as well as you say you are. As you mentioned, I have never left a job before it was finished, but I think in this case Mr. Tuck would understand why I would need to go back home. The job is going pretty fast, but I don't......

I put the letter all back together and handed it to Mama to stick back in the envelope. I still felt a warm glow from Daddy telling Mama he was proud of me. AND, I couldn't help but be excited about the idea of a baby. Maybe we might even get a little brother. Mama broke up my daydreaming.

"Ada Joyce, would you like to iron these little sugar sacks that I have bleached in the sun? Maybe you girls would even like to help me make some baby things?"

I nodded. I had learned to milk. I was going to have a part in the program. I had learned to help care for the garden and take care of the chickens. Now maybe I would learn to sew.

Chapter Eight: May 1937

Each day after school we practiced for the program. On the Friday of the program, Mr. Whipple rang the bell early.

"All right, we have practiced the program until we can get through it with no mistakes. Now if everyone will get home and help do the chores your folks have for you, you can be back here in time for the beginning of the program. Now, I don't want anyone late!"

After chores, Ruthie and I hurried back to school since all the students in the program were supposed to be on the benches behind the curtain ten minutes before time for the program to start. Mama was coming with the Morgans. When we arrived, the only other students there were Johnnie and his little brother.

Johnnie was helping Mr. Whipple and already had one gasoline lamp lit. He took the other lamp outside to fill with gasoline, then brought it back and Mr. Whipple tied two new white silky mantles on. Johnnie pumped it full of air with the little pump built into the base of the lamp. Mr. Whipple then struck a match to the two mantles that shrank into two bright white balls, throwing a brilliant light into the room.

"Johnnie, untie the pulley rope, please, and let it down so we can hook the lamp to it and raise it up high above everyone's head," Mr. Whipple said. Mr. Whipple grabbed the descending pulley and hooked the handle of the lamp over the hook, and Johnnie lifted it towards the ceiling.

"Oh no!" Mr. Whipple said, looking up to where the lamp now hung. "I thought I had killed all the miller bugs!"

Two miller bugs had flitted around too close to the light and zoomed into the mantles, not only committing suicide, but also tearing the mantles to smithereens. The lamp flared briefly, then went out.

"Will we have to call off the program and have it in the day time?" I asked.

"If we don't have some other mantles, we'll have to postpone the program," Mr. Whipple said. But Mrs. Whipple smiled sweetly and handed him two more mantles she had stashed in her desk drawer.

Mr. Whipple again tied the mantles on. This time, with the last of the millers dead, everything went off without a hitch. Soon parents filled the students' seats and waited for the program to begin.

Mr. Whipple stepped from behind the curtains to welcome the parents. "Good evening, parents and friends. We have a great program for you tonight. All of the students have been working hard to make this program the very best it can be. You should all be very proud of your children. They have outdone themselves."

He then announced the first thing on the program, which was my reading, "Ada Joyce, Did You Pass?" My knees were shaking when I walked on to the stage, but I decided to act brave so maybe I would get to feeling that way, and sure enough, it worked by the time I got to the last line, "The merry birds paused just to ask, 'Ada Joyce, did you pass?'" I enjoyed looking at the people there, especially Mama who was smiling from ear to ear.

The next performance was the play, *"Say Hello to Summer,"* which was a school having a program, and I was the teacher who called on the kids for poems, readings, and songs. Everyone liked it, especially the parents of the students performing. There was only one slip up, and that was when Johnnie's little brother Pee Wee, forgot his part, and his mom told him what to say next from the audience. Pee Wee couldn't hear her and said, "What?" real loud, and she repeated it louder this time. Everybody snickered and shy little Pee Wee turned pink as a tulip.

The final act of the program was, *"Dance of the Spring Flowers."* Ruthie looked cute with the white petals around her face and so did the other girls, each one wearing different colored petals to represent their flower. The dance was going real smooth until the buttercup stumbled into the daisy and she fell against the bluebell, who knocked the sunflower off the stage. Mrs. Whipple rushed to see if anyone was hurt, but they were all giggling in embarrassment. The audience stood up clapping and laughing like that was the best part of the whole program. No one was in a hurry to go home. Neighbors did not get to see and visit every day. Mrs. Whipple passed out cookies to everyone, making it seem even more like a party.

Mama hugged Ruthie and me and said, "I sure wish Daddy could have seen you girls tonight. He'd have been so proud!"

Mrs. Whipple's sister, Adeline, was visiting from Goodwell where the college was already out for the summer. When she heard Mama say that, she told her. "Mrs. Johnson, I have three more pictures to take on my roll of film. I have never tried to take pictures at night, but I think if one of the men will move that lamp close, and we can get those little girls to line up, I will be able to take pictures of those cute little flowers. I'd like one of those myself, so I'll try to take two."

"Now, don't you go running off, I want to get a picture of you, too," she told me. "With any luck, we'll have pictures of both of you when your daddy gets home."

So after we got our pictures taken, we went to join the other kids who were playing, "Who Came Near Me?" at the other side of the room. That was a game the teachers had taught us to make us practice good English. Before too long, we heard Mama call to tell us the Morgans were ready to go home, and we'd better hurry!

The following day Mama brought out her fancy woven picnic basket for us to take to the last of school luncheon. She packed it with chicken salad, cinnamon rolls, and a loaf of her good homemade bread. She even put in a jar of dill pickles from the cellar. The basket also held folding tin cups, tin plates, and even metal forks and spoons. Mama's students had given her the picnic basket as a gift when she taught school before she and Daddy were married.

We carried the basket between us, and we talked so much on the way we didn't even notice how heavy it was. Mama stayed home as she said she was a little tired and was going to lie down and rest a bit after she finished the morning work.

We arrived at school and found that Mr. Whipple and some of the big boys had brought boards from the storage shed and laid them on top of desks to form a big table. Mrs. Whipple flipped two of her sheets on top of the boards, and Ruthie and I set the things we brought for the dinner on it. Mrs. Whitmarsh sent a big jar of canned beet pickles and a jar of watermelon preserves. There was baked and fried chicken, ham, homemade bread, potato salad, macaroni and cheese, and a lot of other good stuff. Ruthie and I ate out of the tin plates and put our water in the tin cups. We felt fancy. Someone's Mom brought a big chocolate cake that disappeared so fast you'd think the wind blew it away.

Afterwards, we gathered up the food and covered it with one of the sheets so the flies wouldn't eat it all up, then we joined the boys and smaller girls at play. We played *Drop the Handkerchief, Two Deep, Red Rover,* and *Beanbag Throw*. Some played *Two In and One Out* at the basketball goal, and I joined them. Ruthie played hopscotch with the girls in her class.

Mrs. Whipple gathered the little ones up and said it was story time and she would read to them. We big kids played *Work Up,* which was a baseball game that doesn't have two teams. When one person made an out, he had to go to right field and all the rest of the kids "worked up" from field positions to being a baseman, the pitcher, catcher, and finally one of three batters. When everyone had a chance to be batter, Mr. Whipple said it was about time for school to close and told us kids we could go home. I was glad it was a little earlier than we usually got out of school because Mama had told us to look again for the turkey hen.

I gave the remainder of our jar of pickles to Mrs. Whipple, and stacked the tin plates, and cups in the basket, then called Ruthie, and we headed for home. The basket was a lot lighter without the food, especially the pickles. The tin cups and plates rattled as we swung the basket between us.

We crawled through the fence into our back pasture but hadn't picked up the basket yet when we heard the turkey clucking softly. We scooted quietly to the bank of the draw and sure enough, there she was, down in the bottom with several little turkey poults busy scratching in the dirt beside her.

"Look, Ada Joyce. Is that a dog or a coyote up on that bank?" Ruthie pointed.

"Oh, Ruthie, that's a coyote. He's after those turkeys. Run and get Mama. I'll stay here and guard them."

Ruthie hightailed it for the house, and I looked around for something to throw at the coyote, because, so far, he had ignored me, giving full attention to the little family below. He stealthily eased forward on his belly, hunkered low so he wouldn't be discovered. I found some rocks and threw them, but they were just about the size of marbles, and I threw short. That did not even faze him in his quest for a turkey dinner.

The coyote slunk closer to the turkeys, intent on his prey. A limb was sticking out of the ground so I tried to pull it up, but I could not get it to budge. I pulled at the limb, but no luck, it was buried too deep. The hen, sensing danger, jerked her head back and forth, calling in worried tones for her poults to stay with her.

The coyote had crept up until the turkeys were only a few feet away. He crouched ready to spring. The picnic basket sat there, Mama's pride and joy; it was my last hope, and I had to use it. I grabbed it and flung it with all the strength I could summon. The basket landed between the coyote and the turkeys. The lid flew open with a splintering sound. Cups, silverware, and plates clamored together as they spilled over the ground. One plate rolled towards the coyote as if determined to do its part to protect the little poults. *That* got his attention. Faster than anything, that coyote whirled around and hightailed himself over the hill, gone from sight in a second.

Mama, Ruthie, and Ole Shep arrived just then. "Oh, the coyote's gone!" Mama said breathlessly.

"Mama, I busted your picnic basket," I told her. "I threw it at the coyote."

But Mama was busy counting, "There's nine of them. Bibby is a great mother, but she needs us more than she thinks she does. We have to get these poults to the house and in a pen. That old coyote won't give up." Talking softly to Bibby to calm her down, Mama reached into her apron pocket and dropped four or five dry curds of cottage cheese. Bibby called her babies to come share the feast, and Mama started backing slowly toward the house, dropping bits of cheese just often enough to keep Bibby following with her babies close behind.

As for Ruthie and me, we picked up the basket, which was battered and scuffed now. We gathered the scattered cups and plates, packing them back in the basket, and fell in a few feet behind Mama and Bibby and their entourage. Ole Shep stood back quietly so as not to excite the baby poults, but I know he was prepared to try to round them up if they scattered.

The turkeys would be an important part of the family's income in the fall. Mama depended on the sale of the turkeys to buy some clothes for us, and also to help "Santa" fill our Christmas stockings. We were proud of ourselves as we brought up the rear of the happy parade.

Chapter Nine: July 1937

"Girls, gather the plums as you come to them," Mama said, "Don't pick just easy-to-reach ones. It's easier to make a clean sweep, if you can. Ruthie, you can get the low ones. Ada Joyce can reach the higher ones. Shep, go chase rabbits; you're in the way."

We were in the sandhill plum patch at Fulton Creek, two miles west of our house. We had started our picking an hour ago, but now the sun beat down on us, getting hotter by the minute. I pulled off my bonnet and swiped my skirt tail across my sweaty face. Putting my slat-bonnet back on my head, I reached for a cluster of plums on a high branch.

"Ouch," I hollered, "that branch jabbed me!"

"They'll do that," Mama said, "Not only the branches stick, but you just know they're full of chiggers, too." Just then, Ole Shep jumped up and began barking into the plum thicket as though he could see those chiggers. "Course, there's not a lot we can do about them, except to get a saltwater bath as soon as we can. At first they just itch and sting, but if we don't get them off in a hurry, they will bury themselves under our hides, and we'll have some real sore places in spite of everything we doctor them with."

"I don't think I have any," Ruthie said, "least I don't see any."

"Honey, they're hard to see, just a little round red dot." Mama told her. "Do you girls remember the song I taught you about a chigger?"

Ruthie and I started giggling. We remembered the song. "Sing it. Sing it." We said together.

Mama kept picking but began to sing right then:
"Oh there was a little chigger
and he wasn't any bigger
Than the point of a very small pin,
but the bump that he raises,
Just itches like blazes,
and that's where the rub comes in."

(Ruthie and I joined her on the chorus, then Ole Shep started howling, acting like he was tenor of the quartette.)

"Comes in. Comes in.
Oh that's where the rub comes in.
The bump that he raises,
Just itches like blazes,
And that's where the rub comes in."

"Let's sing it again, Mama." Ruthie said. So we did. We liked it when Mama sang. It made the work go faster and was almost fun.

Ruthie and I emptied our buckets into the tub. One of Mama's washtubs sat katy-wampus in the little red wagon. Because the tub was wider than the wagon, one side rested in the wagon bottom and the other slanted up and extended several inches over the other side. It shouldn't tip over though, if I was careful when I pulled it home.

"Bet I can get my bucket filled before you get yours," Ruthie told me.

"Okay, Ruthie. It's a race," I answered, not mentioning that my bucket held twice as many plums as the little syrup bucket she carried.

After all, she was still a little kid. Besides, the time would go faster if we could keep our minds off the chiggers, the scratchy bushes, and the flies buzzing around our faces. The hot sun beat down on us, making little rivers of sweat roll down our faces and drip onto our shirts.

Finally, the tub was filled as much as we dared fill it, plus the two larger buckets, and Ruthie's little bucket were full of plums. Mama dipped some fresh water from the creek into the water jar we had brought along. She wet the dishtowel she had around it so it would help keep the water cool. Then she lifted a two-gallon bucket in each hand. "Ready for the trip home?" she asked.

"Mama, those are too heavy for you," I said. "Let's pour a few more of your plums into the wagon and make the buckets lighter for you to carry." I grabbed the wagon's handle with my right hand and picked up Ruthie's bucket with my left.

"Ruthie, I'll carry your plums home. Help push on the back of the wagon while I try to get it up out of here and get on level ground."

The black handle of the wagon dug into my hand as I pulled its heavy load out of the low area where the plum bushes grew. We were all so tired that we didn't waste energy trying to talk, even Ruthie was quiet, and she is usually a chatterbox. I tugged the heavy load towards home.

We had only gone about a half mile when I said, "My mouth feels like it is stuffed with cotton. I'll bet I'm not the only one who is dry." I picked up the water jar that had rattled in the wagon beside the tub and poured a drink into the lid and handed it to Mama. I took a long swig and spewed it out. "Ugh, this water is as hot as water out of the tea kettle," I said, "but at least it's wet."

" Ruthie, do you want a drink?" I asked her handing her the jar. We started on after she had wet her mouth a little.

The long sides of my bonnet hovered around my face, cutting off any breeze there might be, and I didn't think there was any. I pushed my bonnet back until it hung behind me, held by its ties around my neck. Sweat run down my back, and my dress stuck to me. I was hot. I was tired. I was miserable. I had to take it out on somebody.

"Betty Ruth, can't you push any harder? If we don't hurry, we'll never catch up with Mama. She'll be at the house and have her plums canned before we even make it past the barn. I think you've been riding on the wagon instead of pushing it."

Ruthie giggled like I'd said something funny. That's what makes me the maddest about my little sister. She acts like the whole world is a picnic and everybody has a bucket of fried chicken and is just aching to give her a big drumstick. She just knows everyone loves her, and the part that makes me the most jealous is, that they do.

I nearly fell forward as the wagon lurched. That little mutt had been riding on the wagon ! I turned to chew her out, but then caught sight of Mama as she looked back, smiled, and stopped to wait for us. She was happy that we found so many plums. Last week when she got off the phone from telling Aunt Osa about finding the plum thicket loaded with gallons of sandhill plums, while we were hunting for the turkey, she said that Aunt Osa asked if we could pick some for her, too.

"Since she runs the post office and can't get away, she said she would give you girls two dollars a bucket to pick plums for her. The four dollars you earned would get your dress material out of lay-away at Ragsdale's store."

I was thinking of that now as we hurried to catch up with Mama. As we reached her, she started singing,

"Captain Jinx of the Horse Marines,
Feeds his horses corn and beans,"

(We tried matching her steps to the lively tune.)

"Swings his lady with all his might,
For that's the style of the Army."

Normally, Mama sang while she walked, and usually would act like she was marching, but she couldn't be quite so frisky now that she was so old, thirty-two, *and* expecting a baby, plus weighed down with two buckets of plums.

"Captain Jinx..." she stopped and asked us girls, now walking beside her. "Did I ever tell you girls where I learned that song?"

"Tell us." We urged.

"Well, when Daddy and I were courting, we used to sing that song as a party game."

"Party game?" I asked.

"Yes. Several young couples would get out in the yard and sing songs and sashay around while we sang. We had lots of them. "Skip to My Lou", "Shoo Fly, Shoo", "Happy Was A Miller Boy", were some of them."

She chuckled now to herself. "We'd sing those songs and run around, sashaying here and there, swinging each other and changing partners. Our folks were pretty strict, but Grandma Johnson was really strict. It was okay as long as we sang while we twirled around, but if someone fired up a fiddle, and the singing stopped, Grandma Johnson, or some other good lady, would storm out of the house and tell us we were not going to dance, as, "dancing was the devil's snare." Mama chuckled and began again.

"Captain Jinx got drunk one night,
The gentleman passes to the right.
Swing that lady with all your might,
For that's the style of the Army."

I looked up in surprise to realize we were home. Mama held the bottom barbed wire down with her foot letting me go through, then I turned and did the same for her as she passed the plums through the fence and followed.

"Ruthie, turn the wagon handle round a little more, so I can pull it through to this side." I said.

A big jackrabbit jumped up from the shade of a post and went bounding away, Ole Shep hot on his heels. Ruthie ignored me and watched Shep and the rabbit until Shep gave up the chase and ran back to us.

Ruthie took a quick look at Mama and, deciding she wasn't looking, stuck out her tongue and crossed her eyes at me for bossing her. But she put the handle of the wagon within my reach, and I pulled it under and through while Mama held the bottom wire up.

We put part of the plums into the cellar but kept those for Aunt Osa in the house, so they would be handy to get this afternoon when she came to pick them up.

"Ada Joyce, hurry and fill the tubs with cold water. I'll fix us a bite to eat while you girls are washing off, then I'll get my bath. Take the water down to the hogs after you're through. The garden is doing so good I don't want to dump any salt water on it."

I filled the tubs with cold water, and Mama put a cup a salt in each one. Ruthie and I washed off, even dunking our heads under the water just in case. After I carried the water to the hogs, one tub at a time in the little red wagon, I filled up a tub for Mama, then went to the house where she had already given Ruthie a glass of milk and a slice of homemade bread, with an egg beaten up and fried flat riding on top of it. She was making one for me just like it. We ate while Mama took her salt-water bath.

She came into the kitchen, drying her long hair on a bath towel. "If you girls are as tired as I am, you are ready for a rest. I'm going to lie down for a while, and I'll bet you girls need to rest and try to cool off some, too."

I did not plan to sleep. I was going to start at the first of my *Heidi* book again, since I didn't get to read much anymore. There was nothing else to read but what was left of the old Sears and Roebuck catalog out in the outhouse.

The telephone rang, three shorts and one long. That was ours. "Hello?" Mama answered. "Oh, hello Osa. We haven't been in very long . . . yes, we did. Two buckets . . . Oh, that will be great. So then all of you can come for supper? We'll be tickled to have company, the kids have not had a chance to play in quite a while. . . . . see you this evening then."

Mama hung up. "She and the boys and Uncle Gerald are all coming." she said.

"Mama, I wished you'd asked her if she could get our dress material out of layaway." I said.

"Oh, she's going to. She offered to get it for us, so she will bring it when they come. She is even going to bring the spring Sears Catalog for you to look at. You can pick out a dress you like, and I'll make you one like it." Mama said.

I changed my plans from reading. I'd rest a little bit, then I'd dust the house. We hadn't dusted in a day or two, but with company coming I thought I would surprise Mama.

About an hour later, Mama called, "Ada Joyce, run to the garden and bring some squash and two heads of cabbage, would you please?"

I went to the garden in a good mood because we always had fun when our cousins Billy and Dale came. They didn't have a wagon, so all four of us kids would go just south of the barn to the little hill in the pasture, and, with two riding the wagon down and two giving a good starting push, we took turns coasting down the hill. Even Ole Shep acts tickled when he sees them coming because that always means he may get a turn in the wagon.

I stepped around the squash vines and found four nice ones just ready to be picked. I cut the two end cabbages, then looked in the cucumbers. Mama's garden was growing good. Since the dirt was not blowing so much this summer, but still enough wind most days to turn the windmill, the garden showed the results of the good care Mama and me gave it. The garden is in the best spot it can be. It gets all the overflow water when the storage tank gets full, besides having a faucet where it can be watered with the hose anytime. A row of asparagus grew along the south edge of the garden. She dug the roots out of the ground in the early spring for us to eat, then later let the asparagus grow up in fern bushes, which she said helped to protect the garden from the winds. She and Daddy had tacked gunnysacks on the fences, too, to break strong winds.

I chuckled when I found five long cucumbers. I'd better have those picked before Dale got here. He loved cucumbers and picked them right out of the garden, eating them peelings and all.

Mama was always horrified. She just knew they would poison him and told him often, "Young man, don't you know those cucumbers are not good for you like they are? You need to soak them at least in salt before they are edible, and adding vinegar first, would be safer."

He always laughed and ate every one he could find. He never ever got a stomachache.

Mother eyed the garden goodies I brought in. "Oh, we will have a feast," she declared. "We'll fix the cucumbers with onions and vinegar. I think we'll cream the squash, and I've got cottage cheese in the wellhouse, and I'll mix up some corn fritters. We've still got light bread so I won't make cornbread since we are going to have corn anyway. Then, I'll make some chocolate gravy for dessert." Mama finished planning her menu out loud. She was as happy company was coming as Ruthie and I were.

I know Mama got lonely with Daddy away. Uncle Gerald was my daddy's brother, and Aunt Osa was my favorite on my daddy's side of the family. She didn't have any girls and always acted like Mama was really lucky because she had us.

"They're coming. They're coming!" Ruthie danced into the house.

"Come on, Ruthie. Let's get the table set."

By the time they got there, we had set the table and were waiting out by the wagon for the car to stop and our cousins to hop out. As soon as Ruthie and I looked at the pretty material, Aunt Osa brought, all us kids headed for the hill. Ole Shep running and circling around us with as much energy as a young pup. Dale pulled the wagon and we three piled in.

Chapter Ten: July, 1937

"Don't, Ada Joyce, don't! Don't kill her!" Ruthie hollered.

"Oh hush, Ruthie. I'm not killing her. I'm just going to hold this old setter's head down with this stick while I get the eggs out from under her. If you think it's so easy to get those eggs, you give it a try."

"When she pecked you and I saw you pick up a stick, I was afraid you were going to kill her," Ruthie said, "and I know Mama is too tired to dress a chicken tonight and I didn't think you learned how yet."

"Ruthie, don't you think I have a lick of sense? I KNOW Mama's too tired to dress a chicken. I'm tired, too, and I'm not old like Mama and, besides that, she's expecting."

Mama does not usually let on like she's tired, but tonight after milking when I asked her if she would like to rest and that I could do the rest of the chores by myself, she admitted she had gone about as far as she could, that she was really ready for a rest. She said she'd strain the milk while I gathered the eggs and watered the chickens. So I came on out to take care of the chickens.

Two Leghorn hens flew off the nests, cackling wildly. Those Leghorns might think they were setters, but Leghorns don't ever take their mothering seriously like Mama's beady-eyed Rhode Island Reds. Those are the only kind she trusts to set on her to precious turkey eggs, and they make wonderful mothers after the eggs hatch. It is funny to watch them. They still scratch for worms and call the young, long after the turkeys have passed them in size and the hens are standing in their 'babies' shadows.

I finished gathering eggs from the now empty nests, and my thoughts went back over the day and what we had accomplished.

Right after we finished the morning chores, Mama told me to go to the cellar and get the jars ready for canning. I wasn't crazy about going into the cellar. Its' spooky. The walls and floor are dirt, with some boards and dirt put over the top. Besides dirt sifting in every time the wind blew, spiders spun their webs in the corners and between the rows of wooden shelves that Daddy had built along the east wall to hold

Mama's canned goods. Yesterday, I had seen a snakeskin hanging off the edge of a shelf, but the *jars* had to be brought out of the cellar so we could put the winter supply of food in them.

I upended the jars and knocked the dirt out, then wiped the dust off the outside of the jars. I carried them up the cellar steps, six jars at a time, and set them in the little wagon that I had parked by the door of the cellar. When I got a wagon load, I took them out to the garden to wash them off with the hose, so any run off water would irrigate the garden plants. After I got the jars as clean as I could with cold water, I pulled them to the house and doused them in a tub of hot, soapy water. Last, Mama helped me rinse and scald them with hot water to sterilize them.

During the time I was getting the jars from the cellar and washing them outside, Mama sorted and stemmed the plums. She then rinsed them and put them in kettles, along with some sugar and water to cover. She placed the pots on the burners for the ripe fruit to cook.

It was an all-afternoon's chore to cook the plums, then transfer the hot fruit into hot scalded jars, and seal with sterilized lids. The hot sweet steam almost felt too thick to breathe as it filled the kitchen. Our dresses stuck to our bodies like we had glue poured down our necks. My job was to stir the bubbling red fruit with a long wooden spoon. Every little bit, we dipped washrags in cool water and washed our faces to cool off and wrapped wet rags around our necks. Finally, we lined up the jars of red fruit, wiped off the outside, and sat down to rest a minute and admire our work.

"The jars will be cool tomorrow, and I will need you to take them to the cellar and arrange them on the shelves." Mama said.

Mama was too tired to go help with the chores, but she insisted. "I'll help with the milking, then soon we can both rest."

So we did do the milking, but while I took care of the chickens, I hoped she was resting in the house. However, it seemed like she could always find something to do.

"Ada Joyce." Ruthie's voice brought me back from my wool gathering to my egg gathering. "Are we through? Can I take the eggs to the house?"

"Sure, Ruthie, and put the cornbread and milk on the table, then we can eat supper and go to bed early. Now don't drop them," I warned her.

Flashing her sweet little grin, Ruthie left, carefully carrying the lard bucket of fresh eggs.

I took a water bucket and went to the horse tank to get water for the chickens. I dipped the bucket into the water, slapping back flat green pancake moss that was floating on top. I sat the full bucket down and splashed water on my face. Would it ever cool off? It wasn't so bad working, now that evening was here, but earlier in the day the heat caused rippling waves along the tops of the hills, almost like they were traveling. I picked up the water and started towards the hen house.

"Ada Joyce. Ada Joyce! Come quick. Mama's dead!" Ruthie came flying toward me. " Hurry, Mama's dead."

The bucket dropped to the ground as I took out after Ruthie. She jerked open the screen door, and I ran past her into the living room where Mama lay crumpled on the grey and white linoleum with the pink roses. Mama looked white as Old Mrs. Tilton when she lay in her grey coffin with real pink roses around her.

I ran to Mama and lay my hand on her chest; the easy rise and fall let me know that she had only fainted. Relief washed over me, and I began to bawl.

"Betty Ruth, go get a cold wash cloth." She came bringing cold water in the wash pan. "Now go get a pillow off Mama's bed while I bath her face." I dipped the washcloth in cold water and slowly wiped Mama's face. Ruthie returned with the pillow, and we slipped it under Mama's head. As we did, her eyes fluttered open and she smiled weakly, saying, "I've got two sweet little nurses."

"Mama do you feel like getting up now and laying on the bed?" I asked her. "I'll finish the work, and you can just rest."

Then I saw the coal oil lamp on the floor. Luckily, the heavy glass base was still in one piece. The chimney was on the table where she had placed it when she started outside to fill the lamp before she fainted.

"I'll fill the lamps, and you can rest." I told her.

"Can you fill them without spilling the coal oil?" she asked.

I wasn't sure because I usually manage to drop or spill something, or fall down, or some dumb thing, but I wasn't going to let on to Mama.

"Oh sure, Mama. That's easy."

We helped Mama to bed, and she lay there with a cold rag on her forehead, still looking pale, but she was breathing quiet and steady.

I left the house to fill the kerosene lamps and finish watering the chickens. Ruthie said, "I'll watch Mama."

When I returned, Betty Ruth put her finger across her mouth to tell me to be quiet, and we both tiptoed out of the room. We went to bed, all thoughts of supper forgotten.

The next morning I slipped into the kitchen for the milk buckets, hoping not to wake Mama.

"Ada Joyce!" Mama called.

I had thought she was asleep. "What Mama?" I asked. "I was hoping you'd still be asleep, and I could slip out and do the milking and let you rest."

"I AM going to let you do the milking this morning, but don't bother to milk old Jersey. It's time she was dried up anyhow. She needs to build her strength for her calf. She is due to calve in about eight weeks."

"You want me to just milk Milly?"

"Yes. Don't let on that you are afraid of her. She is more apt to kick you if she thinks you're scared."

"Oh, I'm not afraid of her." I lied. I doubt if I fooled Mama with my bravery. Why not admit I was quaking? I went whistling out the door as if the job I had ahead of me was as easy for me as it was for Mama.

I drove Milly in without mishap. She put her head in the stanchion to munch on her oats, and I pulled the board shut and put the bar through it. I whistled like Mama does but decided against trying to put the hobbles on her. I placed the milking stool beside her and streams of milk soon pinged against the bottom of the bucket. I had sped up since the beginning of summer, and the rhythm of the milk hitting almost sounded like Mama's milking. Milly stamped a little but was still engrossed in her oats, so I kept drawing the milk out as fast as I could.

The bucket was half full of milk when she whacked me with her cockle-burred tail.

"You IDIOT!" I yelled at her, "Stop that!"

She turned her head to look at me, then hauled off and kicked like a mule. What happened next seemed to be in slow motion. The bucket looped up into the air and landed on my head like a football helmet, the handle hanging down on my chest. Milk streamed down my head plastering my hair to my face. All I could see was white. I pulled the bucket off my head. I was a soppy mess from head to toe. Milly turned towards me with curved lips looking like she smiled at me.

Just then I heard a muffled giggle and looked around to see Ruthie. Her hand covered her mouth, but she could not hide the fact she was laughing so hard her sides were shaking.

"Okay, Ruthie. What's so dad-gummed funny?" I asked her, putting my fists on my hips.

She kept laughing and bent over holding her sides, the bubbling sounds of mirth ringing loud and clear. I thought how silly I must look, and I began to laugh, too. When Ruthie saw I wasn't going to be mad at her, she exploded with laughter, and I couldn't help but join her and so we laughed and giggled until tears streaked down our faces, and we fell into each others arms as we felt the tension of the last few days drain away, with the milk soaking into the barn floor. Milly stared at us like we had lost our senses. I finally got hold of myself, picked up the stool, stuck the bucket under her, and started milking again. "Alright Ole' gal you're gonna get milked whether you like it or not. This is my job for now and we've got to decide which one of us is gonna be boss. I'm voting for me."

At that minute I wished I'd never have to see Milly again, but that was out of the question because, with Mama feeling poorly, I'd have to take over most of the chores. Milking Milly would be my job until Daddy got back from Colorado. In the meantime ONE of us had many lessons to learn. I wasn't sure at that point if it was Milly--or ME.

Chapter Eleven: August 1937

Today was the day of the picnic. It's funny how easy it is to get up early when there is something special coming up, and I did get up early, even before the sun peeped over the flat horizon. I whistled, swinging the milk bucket back and forth on my way to the barn. The wind was blowing some but not much dust was in the air.

After church last Sunday, Mr. Yates told us they were hosting a community last-of-summer picnic and swimming party at their place on the creek on Friday. Ruthie and I waged a real campaign to go, and when Mama finally said, "Maybe, if we have the work done," I took my red crayon and marked a big circle around that date. *Today.*

All of us had worked hard, even Mama who did all the work she could while she sat in the easy chair. I picked green beans and brought them to the house. Mama and Ruthie snapped them while I went back out doors and washed up the jars, getting them ready to start the process of canning them in the pressure cooker. Mama told me each step to do in the canning, but I was the one who dropped the beans in hot water to blanch them before I packed them in the jars as tight as I could. Our pressure cooker cooked seven jars at one time, and as soon as I got seven jars ready to go, Mama told me to put one teaspoon of salt in each jar, then pour boiling water out of the teakettle into each jar of beans and put sterilized lids on them, tightening them before setting the jars in hot water in the bottom of the pressure cooker. That doesn't sound hard to do, but it was mighty hot work.

Now there were twenty-four shining jars of green beans on the cellar shelves. I was proud they were there because of my work. Mama told us yesterday that we had certainly earned a day off to go to the picnic, so the last thing I would need to do is get old Milly milked and out to pasture and the chickens tended.

Milly didn't scare me any more since I had been the only one milking her for some time now. I let her in the stall and fastened her head in the stanchion. She stood as quiet and polite like, as if she had never been a humdinger to milk. She had become used to my ways, and

I found I could tolerate hers. It had been at least a month since she had last tried to kick me. Fact was, I was getting right fond of the skittish miss.

I milked steadily, watching the edge of the milk rise to the top of the bucket. I was a good milker now. I chuckled when I thought about how long it had taken me to get even a quart of milk at the beginning of the summer. I carried the frothy brew to the house and strained it, and then took it to the well house to keep cool. Cutting across the yard to the chicken house, I unfastened the latch of the pen that we locked at night to keep coyotes from stealing the chickens. I fed the chickens and carried fresh water to them, then breathed a sigh of relief because now we could go to the picnic.

When I came to the house, Ruthie was stirring the scrambled eggs, and Mama buttered toast made from her homemade bread. I dipped some water from the water bucket into the wash pan and lathered my hands with some of Mama's lye soap. I turned from drying my hands just as Mama put the stack of toast on the table and scraped scrambled eggs onto our plates. Ruthie poured us each a glass of milk. We took our places at the table.

"Ruthie," Mama said. "I believe it's your time to say the blessing this morning."

We bowed our heads, and Ruthie prayed. "God, thank you for the beautiful day with not much wind or dirt blowing. Please keep it pretty so we can have fun at the picnic. Thank you for the good food we have to eat. Thanks 'specially for Mama letting us go to the picnic, and maybe get in the water. Please bless Grandpa, Grandma, Daddy, and Rina Jo, and please, God, bring Daddy home safe and as soon as you can. Amen."

I was sure God heard because even I realize how Ruthie is so sweet and good that God surely wanted to give her anything she asked for. She couldn't help it that she was pretty, and I wasn't.

"You girls would like to get into the deep water, but since I can't swim, I'd feel so much better if you two will stay in the wading end of the stream. We haven't been swimming all summer, and I don't feel safe letting you in the deep water without Daddy here. He's our family's official lifeguard, you know," Mama chuckled.

Ruthie and I did not say anything. We weren't going to argue with Mama. We both felt safe in deep water, but we did not want to worry her.

We finished eating and I helped Ruthie with the dishes, even if it wasn't my job. Mama packed the food. She had made deviled eggs, fried corn fritters, and picked some red shiny radishes and bright green lettuce from the garden. After she washed them good, she dampened a clean dishtowel and wrapped it around the fresh vegetables to keep them crisp, but best of all, Ruthie had made some thumbprint cookies, and we were taking a batch of them with a dollop of Mama's red plum jelly in each little hollow. The Morgans, our neighbors to the east, were stopping by to get Mama and our food. Ruthie and I were walking on to the schoolhouse to join some other kids who would be riding on the rest of the way in a farm wagon.

"You girls wear old dresses because you'll get them all sandy and muddy in the water." Mama said, "but, please, promise that you won't get in the water until I get there. I know that Daddy taught both of you to swim last summer, but since I can't swim, I would feel safer if you will stay in the shallow end. Please don't go in the water at all, until I get there." She repeated.

Daddy always teased Mama that she reminded him of a mama chicken-hen who set on duck eggs and had hatched two little ducklings who loved to dive into every pond of water they saw, and the mama hen ran frantically back and forth by the side of the water calling to the ducklings about how dangerous their actions were. He said that's the way she acted about Ruthie and me.

Ruthie and I hurried to the schoolhouse where several of the kids had already gathered to ride in a wagon pulled by two horses that one of the older boys had borrowed from his dad. Ben, the driver, sat high on the front seat with Velma, his girl friend, perched up there beside him.

"All aboard," Ben called, flashing Velma a grin. All the kids scampered into the wagon, eager to be on the mile and a half ride to the picnic.

"You kids don't stand up now." Ben called, "You can sit on the hay bales or stand on your knees to look out over the sideboards, but I don't want any of you bouncing out!" He reached out and pulled Velma close to him. Then he clucked his tongue to the horses, and we were off.

We were packed tight, and I counted noses. There was the Vermillion twins, Darrel and Carol; my second cousins, Edith and Willie Jo; then Joy and Eva Clark, and their brothers, Paul and Kenneth. There would be at least twenty more kids waiting for us at the picnic. Lots of the parents were coming as it was too early to plant wheat, and, "if we didn't get rain soon," I'd heard some of the grownups talking that, "it would be much too dry to even think of planting." There had been no row crops harvested except for a few little patches on farms along the creek. People were selling, or had already sold, their cows not used for furnishing milk for their families. But today, everyone would be there to have fun and forget their worries.

Some of the kids were already in the swimming hole. You could hear the yells and splashes even before we got there. Ben stopped the wagon close to the bank above the creek, and the Vermillion twins raced to the edge and went flying over, entering the water with a splash, that flew above the riverbank, sprinkling our shoes and socks.

"Thanks for helping us to get cool," Eva said.

"Come on, Ada Joyce," Ruthie urged, "let's go sit on the bank at the shallow end. We can just hang our feet off."

"No, Ruthie. We promised Mama we wouldn't. Soon, after Mama gets here, we'll get in the water and see if we can catch some of the minnows in our dress tails. Joy and Eva are hollering for us to come and play horseshoes. Look, they've already pounded the stakes in." I took her hand, pulling her towards our friends.

Joy smiled big when we came up. "How' bout me being partners with Ruthie, and you be Eva's partner?" she asked. "That way there will be a big one and little one on each side."

"Sounds great. Who goes first?"

Joy picked a little dried twig and broke it in two. "Whoever gets the longest goes first."

Ruthie got the long one so she would throw first before Eva. Neither of the little girls threw the shoes within six inches of the stake. Joy and I were luckier, soon taking the score to the fifteen points we had agreed on. Joy and Ruthie beat us by one point.

Darrel and Kenneth came running. "We want to take the winners! We want to take the winners!"

"Here, you can take my place," I said to Kenneth, handing him my horseshoe. "I see the Morgan's car coming, and Mama's with them. We need to go help her with the food."

Ruthie and I raced to the car to see which one could get there first. We stopped short as both Mr. and Mrs. Morgan got out, but there was no sign of Mama.

"Where's Mama?"

"Is she sick?"

"No, no." Mrs. Morgan assured us as she handed each of us some food to take to the picnic tables that Mr. Yates had set up. She sent her food along with us. "Your mother said to tell you she has a surprise for you. She said, too, that both of you can get in the shallow end of the water to play. I promised I would keep my eye on you." Mrs. Morgan looked over her shoulder and said, "But your Mother thought it would be best if you didn't get in the water until after your dinner settled."

The fun of getting to play in the water was overshadowed by our disappointment that Mama hadn't come. I thought for sure that she'd be there as she hadn't been anywhere all summer, and I thought since she felt better, she was looking forward to the picnic as much as we were.

We set out food on the table, and Mr. Yates called for everyone to gather around.

"Usually," he said, "usually, we men go first, but today we are going to turn the tables. First, the kids will fill their plates with their Mama's help, if they need it, then the women and men will go next. That way the kids have a little more time for their dinner to settle before they get back in the water. And we'll have a free table to sit around and visit." He chuckled at his own joke. "Now, Brother Hayes, will you ask the blessin'?

Old man Bernard, who's awful deaf, turned to his wife and said loud enough for everyone to hear, "That's the sorriest idee I ever heard of, not lettin' the men go first as the usual custom. What's the world comin' to?"

His Mrs. shushed him and bowed her head when brother Hayes began to pray.

After the "Amen", we kids didn't have to be told twice; we grabbed plates and forks and got in line. Several of the men teased us kids, "Save some of that fried chicken for me."

"Hey, Scooter, do you need sideboards on that plate?"

"Don't make off with all that rhubarb pie. That's my favorite kind," Mr. Vermillion hollered.

The boys enjoyed their kidding. "Ah Mr. Charley, there's enough for an Army."

We girls were tickled that we got special treatment for a change and not have to eat just the backs and wings of the chicken like we usually do, though we tried to act polite and only take two pieces of chicken.

Mrs. Morgan helped Ruthie fill her plate, and I filled mine, then several of us girls took our plates over to eat under the mulberry trees. After we finished, we played "Handkerchief Fortunetelling." The rules were that one girl twist a hanky, not letting anyone see any part of it but the corners. She then asks questions like, "Do you have a secret boy friend?" or, "Did you put the lizard in Mr. Whipple's desk?" The other girl takes hold of two corners of the hanky and pulls it free. If she picks the two corners on the same side of the hanky, the answer is "No," but if the corners she pulls are catty-cornered, that means, "Yes." Then everybody laughs and teases her.

First off, Joy asked me, "Has Johnnie ever kissed you in the cloak room?" I pulled the corners, and it came out "Yes." All the time I let them think the answer was really, "No." Only my cousin, Willie Jo, knew the truth, and she was not going to tell on me.

Our game was interrupted by wild yelling from the boys leaving their horseshoe games, yelling "Swim, swim, swim," as they followed the leader over the riverbank and into the water, one right after another. Most of the girls followed close behind.

"Ruthie, I'll go ask Mrs. Morgan if it is all right for us to get in the water now. Wait here until I get back," I said, and ran over to a bunch of women who were visiting. Mrs. Morgan saw me coming and answered my question before I asked.

"Yes, Honey. You can get in now. I'll be right here watching you."

Willie Jo, Joy, and Eva stayed with us where the water was only about eight inches deep. The water felt cold, but it was so clear we could see the sandy bottom. The little minnows, some with shiny silver backs and others striped from head to tail, were playing in the water, darting first in the sunshine, then in the shade of the tall grasses, almost seeming to be playing a game of tag.

We ran back and forth splashing water onto our dresses, and cooling off fast. We cupped our dress tails in the water trying to scoop up the minnows.

"Let's see if we can herd most of them to the other end of the little pool. If we all get in a row and hold our skirts as far in the water as we can, bet we can get most of the minnows to go to the other end," Ruthie said. "Kind of like a rabbit drive." She added.

So we lined up side-by-side and each stooped and held our skirts as far down into the water as we could. Sure enough, the little minnows scurried to avoid our homemade seine, but we were heading most of them to a bunch in the little pen that we had dug for them out of the sand.

"What's going on? You having a cattle drive?" We heard a familiar voice.

"Daddy!"

We whirled around. There on the riverbank stood our daddy and mama holding hands like school kids, smiles as wide as quarter moons. Ole Shep stood on the other side looking for all the world like he was laughing, too.

"Daddy!" Ruthie and I hollered in unison again, and clawed our way straight up to them, each determined to get the first hug.

Daddy swooped us up, one in each arm. You'd thought we didn't weigh more than twenty pounds, each. We kissed him on the cheek at the same time, and then he gave us bunches of kisses.

"Now," he said, "are we going to stand here hugging and kissing all day, or are we going to swim?"

"Swim. Swim." We hollered. With that, Daddy, Ruthie, and I, ran and jumped in the deep end. We dived and had races and dunked each other and dived some more. "Look. Daddy. Look at me!" Both Ruthie and I tried to show off for Daddy. I think he had a lot of fun, even though he had to stop a little while to visit with the neighbors he had not seen all summer. Too soon, the sun dropped in the West, and we all loaded in our car with the remains of the picnic around us and headed for home.

Even good days have to end. That night, we sat, contented, around our table, talking over how much fun we'd had that day. Ruthie was playing with the little celluloid doll that Daddy brought her.

Then Daddy reached over and gently tugged on my hair.

"And you, Ada Joyce. You are something! Mama has told me how Dr. Smith made her stay off her feet and how you took over and did the work all by yourself instead of calling me. You all made a big sacrifice. You know I would have been home if I had known she was sick. I'd have stayed home in the first place had I known a new baby was coming. It's worked out fine, and because you didn't let me know, we have a winter's supply of beans, flour, sugar and other stuff. Best of all we even got a job building Mr. Tuck's neighbor's barn, and now we even have the money for the land payment, and I brought you a little something, too." With that, Daddy reached behind him and brought out three books. They weren't new, but they were nice.

"I told Mrs. Tuck's how you liked to read, and she had some books she told me to give you. She said these had been her kids when they were younger." He handed me a book frayed around the edges of the binding but that still looked real interesting, called <u>Millions of Cats</u>. Another one looked like it was for kids about Ruthie's age called <u>The Little Engine that Could</u>.

"Oh, Daddy. Thank you! And a dictionary! I've always wanted a dictionary." I hugged it to me, pleased that Daddy had noticed my work and brought me presents!

I glanced at Ruthie, and she looked as pleased that Daddy was bragging on me as if it was her he was praising.

"Ruthie did a lot, too, Daddy. Mama taught her how to cook a lot of good stuff. Doesn't take her ten minutes to do the dishes, and she dusts and sweeps better than I can. Yep, Ruthie has grown up a lot this summer." I looked over at Mama, who was smiling at me like she wanted to say something.

Oh I get it. I grew up a lot this year, too.

The dirt storms weren't over. The Depression had not lifted, but there was food stored for winter, a little money for the mortgage. Mama was feeling better, and we would soon have a new brother or sister. There were new books to read, but best of all, Daddy was home and the family was together again.

Tonight, the Matthew Johnson family, in Beaver County, Oklahoma, felt as wealthy as the Van Aster Bilts of New York City.

CPSIA information can be obtained at www.ICGtesting.com
Printed in the USA
LVOW130808271012

304537LV00004B/2/P